FORBIDDEN PLEASURES

DOCTOR EROTICA

Getting My Prescription Filled By The Doctor

Everlette Saunders

© 2015

Table Of Contents:

Chapter 1: The Appointment

       The last thing Erin Blackmore wanted to do was go to the doctor for the third time in one month. She was in her second year of college at Penn State and she had way more important things to be doing than wasting her time in the waiting room at the doctor's office. Things like partying, drinking, sleeping with her boyfriend and maybe even studying- if she could fit it in. Erin loved college but not because of her classes. She was studying psychology but she was not doing very well in any one of her five courses. She wasn't failing, but her marks were well below what her parents would approve of. Her lack of interest in school stemmed from the fact that she was spending virtually all of her time with her boyfriend Shawn. Shawn was in his final year at Penn state and his motivation towards school had drastically deteriorated. All he seemed to care about was drinking, partying and having sex. Erin loved all of those things too, but she did wish her grades were a little big better. The thought of facing her parents over Christmas break with bad marks was heavily weighing on her.

       Erin was on the bus and she was about ten minutes away from the doctor's office. The sound of the latest popular hip hop song started blaring from her pocket and she promptly picked it up and answered it, seeing on the caller ID that it was Shawn.

"Hey Shawn, I'm just on the bus"

"Hey Erin, I won't keep you long. Dane is having a party tonight and I just wanted to see if you'd like to go"

"That sounds pretty good but I'm not sure. I've got a quiz tomorrow and I have that big paper due at the end of the month"

"Whatever babe, that stuff can wait. This party is going to be unreal"

"Hmm, I don't know, I'll think about it while I sit in the waiting room at the doctors office for an ungodly amount of time, haha"

"Yeah, it probably will take a long time. Call me later?"

"Yes, I'll call you later. Love you babe, see ya"

      The bus stopped about a block away from the doctor's office and Erin hopped off and started to walk. She was a little bit embarrassed about what she was wearing under her winter coat, a thin black tank top that made her breasts look enormous. To top it off she was wearing the tightest sweatpants she owned, which made her bum look fantastic. She had been with Shawn the night before and had forgotten about her appointment when she went to class that day. Her doctor was nearly a senior citizen and she didn't want him checking her out during her appointment. When she walked into the doctor's office the secretary asked her what she needed and told her to take a seat. She was an old grouchy woman and Erin was always surprised to see her still working as she figured she was due to retire any day now. Erin told the secretary that she just wanted a quick checkup and then proceeded to the waiting area.

      She plopped herself into a chair, crossed her legs and picked up a Cosmo magazine that was sitting on the table in front of her. She knew that she was probably going to have to wait a while, but this was normal and expected. Erin never understood why doctors couldn't be more punctual and it always frustrated her. She skimmed through the pages of the magazine until she found an interesting article about giving better blowjobs. She knew she should be reading her textbooks but she really wanted to find out the latest data on the percentage of men that prefer swallowing to spitting. She dove into the article and got lost in the steamy words on the page.

Chapter 2: Negative Influences

"Doctor Stone, your next patient is ready for you"

"Aright Martha, can you just give me a minute if it's not urgent"

"Yes, she said she just wants a quick checkup"

"Okay, well I'm just a little bit behind on paperwork so send her to me in about fifteen minutes"

"Will do"

     Raymond Stone was fresh out of medical school and had just completed his internship at New Minas Health Center. Today was his second day on the job as a licensed doctor and he had taken over for Dr. Laird, who was Erin's regular doctor. Dr. Laird was down with the flu and Ray jumped at the opportunity to get his medical career started when he was asked to fill in. Ray was 28, married and had the world by the horns. He'd had a really great time in college but most of it had been spent in the library. He'd always felt as though he didn't really get to unleash his wild side because he was too busy trying to please his parents. He had been part of a fraternity, but he used it as more of a networking opportunity than a chance to party hard and drink his face off.

     Ray had never necessarily wanted to be a doctor, but his parents were very insistent. He came from a long line of doctors, physicists and lawyers, but his real passion was photography. Nothing on earth gave him more pleasure than walking along a beach and attempting to capture the perfect picture. There was something about the way the waves broke and the mist lingered in the air on a brisk early morning that made Ray smile. He had a top of the line camera and he took it with him everywhere he went, just in case he stumbled upon a perfect moment. The thought of missing a rare moment in time, one where everything aligned perfectly in front of him was a scary thought, so he didn't allow himself the opportunity to miss out. People often laughed at him as he hauled his large camera bag around, but it didn't bother him one bit.

"Stone, you've got a hot one waiting for you. You should hurry it up buddy" Said Phil, another doctor on staff who was one of Rays good friends.

"Really? What does she look like?"

"Tight body, dark hair and green eyes. She's foxy man, the type of girl you want to give a full-body examination to- if you know what I mean."

Phil Cantro had always been a horn dog. Ray had grown up down the street from him. Phil was older and had been best friends with Ray's older brother, but as time passed and when Ray's brother moved away, him and Ray became very close.

"Phil, I don't know how you're not fired yet. It seems like you're always hitting on your patients"

"Ray, if one of my patients wants sexual release I'm going to give it to her. It would be unprofessional of me to not do so"

"Haha, you know no boundaries hey Phil?"

"Why do you think I have soundproof walls in my office? It's not so I can focus while I'm doing my paperwork"

"You've told me before, but remind me, how many women have you had sex with at work?"

"Eight at work, three at my house and four who have called for me to come to their homes and give them a "check up," if you know what I mean"

"You're crazy man, how has nobody caught you yet?"

"Cuz I'm a magician when it comes to the ladies"

"You mean you last about twenty seconds while you're fucking them so nobody has a chance to hear you?"

"Oh fuck off, that's not what I mean. Get in there and see to that sexy patient. She's gorgeous, you'll love her"

With that Ray headed into the examination room and called the secretary and told her to bring in his patient. He pulled out his cell and started playing a game on it as he waited for Erin to arrive.

Chapter 3: Meeting Dr. Stone

When Erin walked into Dr. Stone's office he nearly dropped his cell phone. Phil was right, this girl was on fire. She walked with elegance and grace, swaying from side to side, moving her hips a great deal with every single step. Her dark brown hair fell beautifully around her shoulders and her green eyes were both electric and terrifying. Her breasts were almost gravity defying. Erin extended a hand to Ray and gave him a cute smile.

"Hello, I'm Erin. It's a pleasure to meet you"

Ray nearly froze up. He got tongue tied but eventually gained control and forced out some words.

"Hello Erin, I'm Doctor Stone but you can just call me Ray. I'll be replacing Doctor Laird for the next little while"

"Okay, sounds good Ray" she said with a devilish grin.

Erin took a seat, folded her legs and waited for Ray to speak. She watched him carefully and observed his distinguished features. He had a bold jaw line and stubble on his face that told her he was a very busy man, with little time for shaving. His pale blue eyes were glistening and his arms were thick and muscular.

"So tell me, Erin, what seems to be the problem today"

"Well Doctor, I mean, Ray. I'm just having some issues with my boyfriend"

"Um, are you sure you've really come to the right place for that? I'm a physician, not a psychologist or psychiatrist"

"No not like actual relationship trouble, I mean sexual trouble"

"Oh alright, go on"

"On second thought, are there any female doctors in here I could speak with. I think this is going to be a little awkward"

"Doctor Monroe is here, but she is extremely busy. Erin, you don't need to worry. Doctors have to follow a strict confidentiality code with every single patient. Besides, your regular doctor is a man anyway, so how is this any different?"

"Well doctor Laird has known me forever and he's, well, really old. You on the other hand, I just met and you're not even that much older than me"

"Erin, you have nothing to worry about. You can ask me anything. Get it off your chest" Ray said in a calming tone. He found his eyes wandering down and glancing at her breasts, but he quickly caught himself and regained eye contact.

"Okay, well I've been feeling a little bit sexually frustrated lately" Erin began to open up.

"In what way?" Ray said as he pulled out a pen and pad to jot down some notes.

"Well, I feel like my boyfriends penis isn't any bigger than average, but it really hurts to have sex with him. I think I'm just naturally more tight than a lot of women."

Ray pretended to be writing on his pad, but in reality his heart was racing and his erection was growing.

"Pain during sex isn't a highly uncommon thing for a lot of women. As you said, some women are just naturally more tight than others"

"Wouldn't you think I would just stretch out and get used to it?"

"Well yes, but you're probably a women with a high degree of elasticity in your vagina, which is great for when you have kids" Ray joked trying to make light of the situation. Erin barely cracked a smile.

"I don't even want to think about kids right now. I dunno Doc, sex is supposed to be fun and I'm in college and I can barely enjoy it"

"That's a shame Erin. This next question is not meant to be offensive or intrusive, but do you use a dildo?" As Ray asked the question he began to imagine Erin sliding a thick pink dildo deep into her pussy.

"That's kind of a weird question"

"Erin, it's in no way unprofessional. It's one of the few practical solutions to your problem"

"Yes, I have a small dildo that I use a couple times a week"

"Well, perhaps you should get a slightly larger one and continue trying to increase the size of your dildos until you no longer feel pain during sex"

"I guess that makes sense. It's just so frustrating not being able to have an orgasm"

"You'll get there, Erin, don't worry. Just sit tight for a minute, I'll be right back"

Ray was nearly sweating; he had never been asked questions like this from such a young, sexy woman. He had a wife at home but Erin was way younger and way more in shape. He rushed into Phil's office and interrupted him from his paperwork.

"Phil, this girl is too much"

"Why? What's up?"

"Her problem is that she's too tight... Can you believe that?"

"Jesus, Ray, you just hit the jackpot. What did you tell her?"

"I just told her to start using larger dildos and to be patient"

"You moron, get in there and take care of her yourself"

"Getting fired for fucking a patient isn't exactly how I want to start my medical career"

"Why are you in my office then? You've obviously come for advice"

"No, I just needed to get out of there. I'm fine now, I'll talk to you later"

Chapter 4: Urges

Erin waited patiently for Dr. Stone to return. She found herself daydreaming about him inside of her. He was much older and she knew he was highly experienced. She wanted him to loosen her up, even if it meant a little bit of pain. But she knew it was wrong, he was married and she had a boyfriend- her fantasies would have to remain just that, fantasies.

"Okay Erin, it was great meeting you and I hope I helped you out a bit today," Dr. Stone had returned and was quickly trying to get Erin to leave his office.

"Yes, thank you very much"

"Maybe you could come back next week and we can see how everything is going?" Ray couldn't believe what he had just said, he knew he wanted her to return but he had no intention of vocalizing it. The words just sort of forced themselves out of his mouth.

"Yes that sounds good, same time and place?"

"Yes, I will see you next week. Take care, Erin."

Erin stood and slowly walked out of the office past Ray who was standing in the doorway. Rays eyes followed her movement and he couldn't help but watch her firm ass as she walked away from him. Erin turned around and caught him starring at her and Rays face turned blood red. He walked inside his office and closed the door. Erin giggled to herself as she made her way out of the building. She had never been excited to go to the doctor in her life, but she couldn't help feeling happy about her appointment the following week.

Soon after Erin left, Phil burst into Ray's office and began to interrogate him.

"So what happened?"

"She's going to come back next week for another appointment"

"You're going to give her a physical right?"

"I might examine her, yes"

"You're a lucky bastard, remember though, you're married. You should just pass that patient over to me so I can actually help her out"

"Oh shut up Phil, I know I'm married. You don't have to remind me about my boring home life, I have to deal with that reality enough on a daily basis"

"Well, this is your chance to spice things up a bit"

"Man, I don't know"

"Hell, maybe she's a freak, maybe she'd be down with having both of us at the same time"

"You're nuts"

"I'm serious, I will let you use my office for your next appointment just in case things get a little hot and heavy. Then after a little while I'll come in and we'll see what she says"

"Phil, just let me handle my business. I'm trying to keep things somewhat professional here"

Chapter 5: Live it up

Later that night, Erin went to a party with Shawn. She didn't even really want to go, but he pressured her until she said yes. Once they arrived, Erin quickly found her friend, Cassandra, and they began doing tequila shots and playing beer pong with some other girls. Within an hour Erin was drunk and feeling good; then the gossip came out.

"Cass, you should see my new doctor" Erin said sloppily.

"Haha, I hope he's a little better than Laird. From what you've told me that guy is old and creepy"

"This guy is a young stud, I'm telling you. I couldn't believe it when I first saw him"

"Really, what does he look like?"

"Short dark hair, light blue eyes, very muscular- I know he's got a six pack under his shirt He's tall and his jaw that could cut steel"

"Sounds like a looker"

"Oh Cass, he's unbelievably handsome"

"Thanks for the compliment, babe" Shawn had snuck up behind her and interrupted the juicy conversation.

"Oh hey Shawn, we were just.."

"Save it Erin, who were you talking about?"

"Uh, just this guy from a TV show that we watch"

"I see, well come in the kitchen we're going to play some flip cup"

"Okay, come on Cass, let's go" Erin said as she grabbed Cassandra's hand and led her into the other room.

After a few rounds of flip cup Erin could feel her phone vibrating in her pocket. She stepped away from the group, took as seat on the couch and saw a new text message from an unknown number, the text read: *Erin this is Dr. Ray Stone. Do I have the correct number?* Erin felt her heart beat a little bit faster as she finished reading the message. She was fairly intoxicated and not using her best judgment; she replied: *Yes this is Erin, what's up Dr. handsome?* After she pressed send she could hardly believe what she'd just done, but she was so drunk that she brushed it off and let out a childish giggle. She felt like she was being so bad, hitting on her hot, older doctor. She waited patiently for a reply as she watched Shawn chug a beer. She knew they weren't right for each other; she needed someone older and more successful. After a few minutes she felt her phone vibrate again. She read the message with a smile on her face: *Erin, I don't want to be inappropriate with you. I felt weird searching through your file to get your number, but I just wanted to see if you were doing okay.* Erin promptly replied: *Yes Ray, I'm doing fine. I'm actually taking your advice right now and using a big thick dildo on my tight little pussy.* Erin was even shocked at the lie she had just told, but she didn't regret it at all. About five minutes later Ray replied and Erin was anxious to see what he'd written. *Jesus Erin, you turn me on more than anything. My wife is nearby though and I have to go. I will see you next week. Make sure you get that little pussy nice and warmed up for me.* After reading this, Erin could feel her pussy quiver and become moist. Her heart was racing and she had to sit down on the couch. She mustered up the courage to send one last message: *Ok Doctor, I'll have my pussy nice and warmed up. I want you to give me a full body examination next week.* She slid her phone back into her pocket as Shawn approached the couch.

"Babe, what's up? You being lame tonight?" Shawn asked.

"Screw you Shawn, I'm just tired and I should be studying right now"

"Well then go do it, I'm not making you stay here"

"Well you basically forced me to come"

"Whatever, I'll see you tomorrow, I'm going to finish off this case of beer."

Shawn walked away and Erin went to find Cassandra. Once she found her they said goodbye and Erin headed back to her small residence room that was a couple streets away. She stripped down into her thong and bra and snuggled up under her covers. She grabbed her small dildo and gently began rubbing it against her clit. The thought of Dr. Stone was getting her soaking wet, she couldn't wait to let him fuck her. She started sliding the dildo inside of herself and rubbing her clit with her other hand. She thought of how hard Ray was going to make her cum. She knew that he was experienced and that he probably knew exactly how to please a woman. As she drifted into ecstasy she was overcome by an orgasm. She sank deeper into her bed- totally satisfied, and drifted off to sleep, a smile still on her face.

Chapter 6: The Mix Up

Phil smiled to himself as he put Ray's phone back to where he'd found it, but not before deleting the messages he'd just sent to Erin on Ray's behalf. As he left Ray's office he practically ran into him outside the door.

"Why are you in my office?" Ray asked.

"Uhh, I was just borrowing a pen"

"Bullshit, why are you in here?"

"You can thank me later"

"Fuck off, what were you doing?"

"I pulled Erin's file and just sent a couple messages to her on your behalf, that's all," Phil said nonchalantly.

"YOU WHAT?" Ray screamed.

"Man, calm down. It's okay, she totally wants you"

"That's not the point Phil!"

"That is the point man, you're not happy with your wife at all. You might as well experience something new"

"What did you say and what did she say?"

"Well I just told her that you were checking in on her and then she said that she was using a dildo. She said she was warming up for you next week, even after I said that you had a wife"

"Women love married men, that's just a fact. Did she really say that though?"

"Yes, she did, I wouldn't lie about something this serious"

"You're a bastard, Phil, you know that?"

"We'll see if you say that after Erin's checkup next week." Phil gave him a wink and then walked away.

Ray's heart was beating fast; he hadn't had sex with a new woman in a very long time. In fact, he hadn't had sex at all in a very long time. His wife was always miserable and he was certain she was just with him for the money. He finished filing some paperwork and then headed out to his car. He pressed a button on his key fob and his jet black Audi started up. He got inside and gripped the steering wheel tightly. He stared forward and let out a yell of excitement. He could hardly wait for next week.

Chapter 7: Anticipation is a Bitch

The week went by very slowly for both Ray and Erin. Ray kept himself busy with a constant influx of patients while Erin contemplated how she was going to breakup with Shawn before her appointment. Ray was getting more and more stressed out as the days went by. He so badly wanted to have Erin, but at the same time he didn't want to jeopardize his medical career. He decided that everything would be fine and that he would simply use Phil's office where there was a very small chance of him being caught.

Erin was becoming very good at almost breaking up with Shawn. She was worried that he would get aggressive when she dumped him. He often talked about getting married and she worried that he might lose it if she dumped him. Finally, one night while they were watching a movie in his room, she decided the time was right.

She was lying on Shawn's lap as the movie came to an end. Once the credits started rolling down the screen, Erin took a deep breath and spoke softly.

"Shawn I..... I don't think... I'm just..... Well I'm not happy"

"Not happy? What are you talking about?"

"There's not much to explain, I'm just not happy with you anymore"

"What are you talking about? You seem pretty happy to me most of the time, especially when I'm buying you dinner and god damned jewelry"

"That's not the point Shawn, I buy you shit too"

"Oh yeah, Like what?"

"I got you fucking tickets to that Bulls basketball game last summer and I also pay for gas every time we go on a trip"

"Well whatever, if you're not happy then you can just leave"

"Okay," Erin said as she quickly got off the bed and headed towards the door.

"See ya tomorrow babe," Shawn said in an arrogant tone.

"It's over Shawn, there is no tomorrow," Erin said as she left. She was proud of her swift response and dramatic exit.

"Wait, what? Babe get back here, I'm joking around," Shawn said as he chased her out of the room. Erin didn't turn around and she just kept walking.

"Babe, stop," He said grabbing her arm and spinning her around like they were some sort of dancing couple.

"Get your fucking hands off me," Erin said angrily.

"Don't talk to me like that, you're not leaving me, stop being stupid"

"Oh, so you're going to force me to be with you? I'm not doing this anymore, I'm sick of your shit, it's over," Erin said as she turned and walked away. She waited for Shawn to yell and scream but he didn't say anything. She continued walking at a brisk pace until she was almost at the front door. Just as she reached for the handle she felt something smash her in the side of the head. She fell sideways into the wall and then landed on the floor, looking up to see Shawn standing over her with a bloody, clenched fist. He stood overtop of her and delivered another vicious blow to her left eye.

"You fucking bitch, you think you're just going to walk out on me? You said we were going to be together forever," There was rage in his eyes, a look Erin had never seen before.

She held her hand to her right ear, where Shawn had punched her. She was bleeding and her ear was ringing loudly. She was terrified, but she didn't show it. She slowly stood up, looked Shawn directly in his irate eyes, and spoke.

"Open your mouth one more time and I'll sue you. My uncle Barry will ensure that you don't see daylight for years. I'm leaving, if you ever call, text or speak to me again, then I'll tell everyone how you beat women. Go fuck yourself you pathetic prick." She turned and walked out the front door, slamming it behind her. Shawn never followed and he didn't say another word. Erin couldn't hold her tears anymore, she started crying and called Cassandra. She didn't answer and Erin began crying even harder. Five minutes later, Cassandra called back and Erin answered after one ring.

"Cass, oh my god he fucking hit me," Erin sobbed.

"Who, Shawn?" Cassandra yelled into the phone.

"Yes, Shawn. I broke up with him and he freaked out. He hit me in the head and now I'm bleeding and my ear is swollen"

"Erin, call the police right now. You can't let that bastard get away with this"

"No, I don't want to ruin his life. I'm just going to go to the doctor first thing in the morning, I'll be fine, I just needed to talk to you"

"Erin, come over and we can talk about it more"

"Okay, I'll be there in fifteen minutes."

Erin quickly walked to Cassandra's apartment. Once she let her inside they embraced in a long hug. After a few moments of silence, Erin began to speak.

"Cass, I just want to forget about this night"

"Okay, we don't even have to talk about it anymore. But Christ, your head looks horrible. Your ear is swollen, you have a cut on your head and I think I see a black eye coming"

"I know, you don't need to remind me"

"You should go clean up in the bathroom"

"I will after we chat, but seriously, I don't want to talk about this anymore"

"Sorry, we won't talk about it anymore

"Good, besides there's more important stuff we have to talk about"

"Like what?" Cassandra asked as she ushered Erin to follow her over to the couch.

"Like the hot doctor I'm going to fuck tomorrow"

"WHAT?"

"Yeah, that Ray Stone guy I told you about, remember? The super handsome doctor" Erin said as she plopped herself down on the couch.

"Erin! How old is this guy? I don't really remember, I was pretty drunk when you told me?"

"Dunno, late twenties, maybe thirty"

"Is he married?"

"Yes, but whatever, He wants it"

"You little home wrecker," Cassandra said with a chuckle as she punched Erin lightly on the shoulder.

"Oh stop being dramatic, you've probably done worse"

"No way!"

"Whatever, the point is I'm going to see him tomorrow and we're probably going to fool around"

"And what would give you that idea?"

"Because of what he was texting me last night"

"What did he say?"

"See for yourself," Erin said as she handed Cassandra her phone. Cassandra quickly scrolled through the messages and the expression on her face changed from focused to shocked.

"Jesus Erin, you really didn't hold back huh?"

"I was drunk, whatever. You know what they say, there's truth in drunk words"

"Well this is your decision. If you want to have sex with him and have a good time, go for it girl!"

"Would you do it?"

"If he's as sexy as your saying, then hell yes I would do it!"

"Thanks, I knew I wasn't crazy. Anyways, I should probably get some sleep. You mind if I crash here?"

"No worries girl, anytime."

Erin headed into the bathroom and took a long, warm shower. As she washed her sleek body she kept imagining Dr. Stone in the shower with her. She wondered what he would do to her, how he would have her. The anticipation was killing her. Before she drifted off to sleep she sent Dr. Stone a quick message: *Hey, no need to worry but I'm going to come into your office tomorrow. I had a rough day and I got a little bit hurt. I just need you to look me over quick.* She pressed the send button and fell asleep in seconds.

Chapter 8: No Appointment Necessary

When Erin woke up she quickly checked her phone to find that Dr. Stone had replied only a few hours ago. *Hey Erin, I just finished a long shift at the hospital downtown. I'm actually not going to be at the medical center today because I need to catch up on sleep and return to the hospital in a few hours. I'm really sorry and I hope everything is okay. I also hope that you're still coming in for your appointment next week. Take care.* Erin was overwhelmed with disappointment, but she knew she had to go see a doctor because her ear was not in good shape. She sent Ray a short message: *No worries, Yes I'm definitely still coming to my appointment, don't worry about that. Have a good day handsome.*

She said goodbye to Cassandra and thanked her for her hospitality. She headed down to the main road and jumped on the first bus that was headed to the medical center. When she felt her phone vibrate in her pocket, she knew it was Ray. This whole fantasy was starting to consume her every thought. She felt like a little girl who had fallen in love for the first time again. She read the message and couldn't help but smile: *Glad to hear :) God, you're so beautiful. I can't wait to see you again. Take care!*

This time the messages were actually coming from Ray and not Phil. Ray could barely focus on his job as he was so caught up in his ordeal with Erin. He caught himself staring off into space more than a few times, imagining what he was going to do to Erin when he finally got his hands on her. He could just picture what her perky breasts looked like and her toned, round ass. He couldn't wait to taste her sweet juices.

"Ray, you day dreaming again?" Asked a colleague.

"Shit, sorry Jen I'm just really out of it today. I barely got any sleep and it seems like only a few hours ago that I was leaving this damn hospital"

"That's because you did leave only a few hours ago. Welcome to the medical world pal." Jen Swanson was nice enough, but she could be very condescending at times. Her height didn't seem to match her bossiness or her ego, as she was a very short woman. She was a medical supervisor in the hospital and Ray had to deal with her a lot during his internship. Jen knew her stuff and she wasn't afraid to let people know it. Her extremely short, spiky black hair made her look like someone out of a punk rock band and Ray guessed that she had been a wild anarchist of some sort in high school.

"Yeah, I know I've heard the lecture a million times. Being a doctor is the hardest profession there is," Ray said as he rolled his eyes.

"Yes and you better not forget it Dr. Stone. Now get back to work immediately"

"Yes, understood Dr. Swanson."

Ray began doing his rounds in the hospital, asking all of the nurses if they needed anything for their patients. Once he decided that everything was in order he pulled out his phone and sent Erin a message: *Hey Erin, just wanted to check in. I hope everything goes well today. Keep me informed.* He then went into the bathroom and waited eagerly for a reply. After only a few short minutes Erin responded: *Hey Doctor, I just got off the bus and now I'm in the waiting room. They told me it should be about a 40 minute wait since I don't have an appointment :(I'm meeting with Dr. Cantro so hopefully he can take care of me.* All Ray could think about was how Phil was probably going to make a move on Erin. He quickly sent her a message back: *That sucks about the wait. Phil Cantro is a old friend of mine; you'll be in good hands.* Ray then immediately sent Phil a message: *Phil I swear to God if you try anything on her I'm going to kill you.* Phil replied almost immediately: *Whoa, relax partner. I thought you didn't want her. I wasn't going to try anything but now I might just to piss you off. LOL just kidding don't get your panties in a knot.* Ray left it at that. He wasn't convinced by this message but he would just have to trust Phil.

After a lengthy wait, Erin was finally instructed to enter Phil's office. He greeted her with a handshake, they exchanged names and he told her to take a seat. Erin was surprised to see yet another good looking doctor in the same medical center. Phil's long blonde hair was very intriguing to her and she thought he looked a lot like a strong, rugged Viking.

"So Erin, it seems that you've taken quite the beating; cat fight at the bar?"

"No, I actually dumped my boyfriend and he lost it on me"

"Are you serious? Did you call the police?"

No, I don't want to involve them. I'm fine and I'd rather just move on with my life"

"Erin, that's a very noble thing to do but you really shouldn't let this asshole get away with that. He hurt you pretty bad, I can tell just by looking at you that I'm going to have to drain your ear due to the fluid buildup"

"Doctor Cantro, please just leave it alone. I'm not involving the police. I just want to heal up and move on"

"Very well then, let me grab a pin and I will get that ear drained. I recommend icing that eye as soon as you get home as well."

Phil rolled his chair over to his desk and pulled a pin out of the drawer. He sterilized the pin and rolled back over to Erin.

"Okay, hold still, this may hurt just a bit," Phil said as he slid the pin into Erin's swollen ear. There was a significant amount of fluid in her ear and it took a couple minutes for it to drain completely. Once the procedure was complete, Phil slid his hand down Erin's back and began to rub her softly. Erin offered him a smile but then stood up, thanked him and left the office. On her way back to the bus stop she pulled out her phone and dialed Ray's number, she needed to hear his voice. Unfortunately he didn't answer so she sent him a quick text instead: *Hello sexy, everything went well with Dr. Cantro. He drained my ear and everything seems to be back to normal. I called you so you can call me back later if you want. Can't wait for next week!*

Chapter 9: Sparks Fly

The week seemed to pass in slow motion and Erin could barely stand it. She was happy that her ear was returning to its normal size and that her black eye was subsiding, as she didn't want to scare Ray off; but she figured he's probably seen much worse than a black eye and a swollen ear in his line of duty. During the week she had been texting Ray a fair bit and the anticipation was now more than she could bear. She showed up at the doctor's office forty-five minutes early for her appointment. She sat patiently reading a Cosmo magazine until the secretary told her to head down to Dr. Cantro's office. Erin was confused and disappointed by this as she had planned to meet with Dr. Stone, but she entered the office and was pleased to see Ray sitting in a chair with a big smile on his face.

"Erin, hello, how are you doing?"

"I'm great Doctor Stone, how are you?"

"Please, like I told you, call me Ray"

"But I feel naughty calling you Doctor"

"Then you can say it as much as you like," Ray squirmed in his chair and Erin gave him a dirty smile.

"Why are we in this office?"

"Well there's some work being done in my office, so Phil told me I could share his for the day"

"Nice, how does my face look?"

"You look gorgeous, I can barely tell anything happened to you. Why don't you take a seat on the table and I'll give you a more thorough examination," Erin could see a bulge forming in Dr. Stones pants, she could tell he was starting to get hard just thinking about what was going to happen next.

Erin hopped up onto the table and got comfortable. Ray told her to lie down and she quickly obliged. He walked over to the table with a confident swagger and slowly unbuttoned and removed his shirt. His stethoscope loosely hung around his neck and Erin wondered why he didn't remove it. He leaned in towards her and removed her shirt.

"I'm going to check your heartbeat, is that okay?" He whispered softly in her ear as if he were afraid somebody was listening.

"Yes, don't be alarmed though, I'm not having a heart attack, I'm just nervous"

"Why are you nervous Erin, I'm going to play nice, I promise," He said offering her a friendly smile.

"I know, I just... I just really want you"

"I want you too, and I'm going to have you. It's time for your physical, take off all of your clothes"

Erin stripped down and then resumed her position on the bed. Ray placed the stethoscope on her chest and listened to her rapid heartbeat as he reveled in the beauty of her body. Her curves were immaculate and her long dark hair appeared to be smoother than silk. Her sharp green eyes seemed to stare directly into his soul and his member was growing harder and harder. Erin was nearly shaking with anticipation. She stared into Dr. Stone's eyes, which were as blue as the Caribbean Sea on a hot sunny day. She bit her lip and pressed her breasts together as if to signal him to remove the stethoscope and start pleasuring her. Ray threw the stethoscope to the floor and removed his pants. His body was toned and muscular and his member was stiff and utterly massive. Erin grew nervous at the site of his large cock, knowing that it wasn't going to fit inside of her easily, but she didn't care. She wanted the Ray to have her, no matter how bad it hurt.

"Get onto your stomach and prop your ass up in the air"

"Is my physical about to begin?"

"Yes, I need to feel around inside you a bit and get you nice and wet before I fuck you hard and fast"

Erin's tight pussy was getting wet just from hearing Ray speak. She presented her ass to him and he got behind her and went to work. He gently began massaging her clit and siding one of his fingers deep inside of her. She moaned loudly as her pleasure started to build.

"Jesus, I want to taste your pussy so fucking," He said in a raspy voice. He almost sounded animalistic as he spoke.

"Taste me, lick my pussy until it's wet enough to take your big cock"

"You're such a good patient"

Ray softly started licking her pussy. His licks were long and wet, starting at the top of her pussy and ending directly on her asshole.

"Oh yes, Doctor Stone, do you like the taste of my ass?"

"I love it baby," He responded as he frantically caressed her tiny asshole with his tongue. He then moved back to her clit as he slowly slid a finger into her ass. Erin pulled away as she felt the finger go in, but Ray pulled her back and began moving his finger around inside of her. Erin had never had anything in her ass before but she was starting to enjoy the feeling.

"Erin, your little asshole is so fucking tight. I don't think my cock will ever fit"

"I know, just fuck my pussy Doctor, we'll save my ass for another day."

Ray began fingering her pussy again, this time with a lot more force and speed. He started with one finger, but after a few minutes he was up to three. He pounded his fingers deep into her wet hole as she started to squirm and squeal. Erin knew she was going to cum, she yelled out for the doctor to spank her and he did so- much harder than she anticipated. She leaned into his fingers as he continued thrusting them into her and she found her sweet release. Immediately after she had an orgasm, Ray climbed onto the table and started teasing her wet opening with his throbbing cock.

"Oh put it in me Doctor, let me feel your hardness"

"Can you handle me Erin?"

"Yes, yes give me all of your cock!"

Ray slowly slid inside of her, Erin held her breath and she felt the full extent of his length and girth. It was painful at first, but when his entire cock was inside and he started to pound her, she couldn't get enough.

"Oh yes, fuck me harder Doctor, Harder!"

"Oh yes, take it you dirty fucking girl"

"Fuck my tight little pussy Doctor"

"You're so young and tight, I love it baby"

He rammed his hips into her ass and she felt like he was going to rip her in half. She could feel her pussy stretching wide each time he thrust.

"Get on your knees, suck your juices off my cock,"

He commanded fiercely. Erin obeyed and fell to her knees immediately. Ray stood above her and she looked up at him eagerly. He looked so powerful from this vantage point, so dominating. Erin enveloped his member with her mouth and started licking the head of his penis and jerking his shaft.

"You like tasting your pussy on my cock you dirty whore?"

"Oh yes Doctor I love it," She said, momentarily removing his stiff dick from her mouth.

"Lick my balls, Erin"

"With pleasure"

Erin took both of Ray's large testicles into her mouth and started teasing them with her tongue. She continued jerking him off as she gently sucked on his balls. After a few minutes, Ray lay down on the bed and gestured for Erin to mount him. She got on top of him and slowly sat down on his thick bone. He grabbed onto, wrapping her into a powerful hug as he starting thrusting himself up into her tight vagina. He spanked her as multiple times as he fucked her as hard as he could. She screamed his name and begged for him to cum, she could hardly take anymore of his girth. He announced that he was nearing orgasm and he picked up his pace. Before Erin knew it she could feel Dr. Stone's warm load shoot inside her. He kept thrusting as cum continued shooting out of his cock. When he was satisfied that he had filled Erin up, he pulled his penis out of her. She hopped off the table, spread her legs and held a hand underneath her pussy. Ray's seed came trickling out of her like a fountain and into her hand, there was so much cum and Erin couldn't believe the size of his load. After all the cum had dripped out of her pussy, she looked at the thick cream that was now in her hand. She gave Ray a dirty smile before slurping up every last drop of the warm semen, licking her hand until every last drop was in her mouth. She swallowed it down, reveling in the sweet taste.

"You're such a freak, Erin," Ray said, satisfied to see her swallowing his cum.

"You've got that right," She responded as she started putting her clothes back on.

"That was amazing, did it hurt for you?"

"No it felt amazing, no one has ever gotten me so wet in my life"

"I've never had sex with such a gorgeous girl. You are aware that this has to be our little secret though, right?"

"I know Ray, you're a married man. I'm not some crazy young college girl; I know this isn't going to amount to anything. We're just two people having fun"

"I'm glad you're so understanding. Why don't you go book another appointment for next week and we'll have even more fun?"

"Consider it done."

They shared a passionate kiss and Erin immediately booked another appointment with the secretary. She was so satisfied with what just happened and she couldn't wait to tell Cassandra that she had just had sex with Dr. Stone. Ray couldn't wait to tell Phil either and they had a great afternoon talking about the encounter. Phil convinced Ray to let him join in on the fun the following week. Ray figured that Erin was kinky enough to have two men at the same time and neither one of the men could wait for Erin's next appointment.

Chapter 10: Round Two

The next appointment came surprisingly quickly as far as Erin was concerned. She didn't have to wait for long this time, she had practically just walked in the door when the secretary told her to head to Dr. Cantro's office. When she arrived Dr. Stone was waiting for her.

"Hey, is your office still being renovated?"

"I lied last time, these walls are soundproof, that's why I brought you in here"

"Oh, somebody was being very presumptuous"

"Yeah, sorry. I just didn't want to get caught"

"Understandable I suppose. What's with the soundproof walls?"

"Doctor Cantro likes to make sure nobody can eavesdrop on his conversations with patients. He takes confidentiality very seriously"

"I see. You're looking sexy today Doctor"

"As are you, why don't you get more comfortable? Take those clothes off and let me taste that sweet pussy"

"If you insist Doctor," Erin said as she slowly stripped.

"I'm pretty into photography, do you mind if I take some pictures of you?"

"No way, I don't want pictures of myself on the Internet"

"No, no, I wouldn't do that. I just want to have some beautiful pictures of you. I can send them to you as well. It's a great camera, takes amazing pictures"

"Okay, but just a few"

"Perfect," Said Ray as he took his camera out of the bag.

"Why don't you press your breasts together for me, Erin?"

"Okay, like this?" She said as she squeezed her perky tits against one another. Ray took a few pictures and then continued to instruct her.

"Yes, just like that. Finger yourself for me. I want to watch you pleasure yourself"

"Whatever you say Doctor," She said as she began massaging her clit. Ray was getting hard and Erin knew it.

"Now bend over the table"

"Yeah, you wanna see me from the back?"

"Fuck yeah, Erin. I want to see you from every angle"

Erin bent over the table and arched her back so that her ass was popping out. She licked her finger and slowly started to rub her tight hole.

"Spread your bum for me Erin, let me see that tight little asshole"

"Yes Doctor, whatever you want," She said as she opened her legs wider and pulled her cheeks apart, exposing her ass to Ray. He loved how tight she was. Her asshole was glistening in the light from her saliva. It looked like a little starfish and he wanted to conquer it.

Just then the office door swung open and Phil burst in. Ray tried to act surprised, but he knew it was all part of the plan. Erin jumped to the other side of the table and crouched down, hiding her naked body from view.

"Ray, what the fuck? You didn't lock the door?" She yelled.

"Shit, I'm sorry. Phil what are you doing in here?"

"Ray, this is my office, remember? I figured you two were fucking in here and I wanted to join the party," Phil said with a smile.

"Phil, she's a young lady, not some slut who wants to get double teamed"

"Ray, you don't get to tell me what I will and will not do," Erin said from across the room.

"Oh, you would have both of us?" Ray asked eagerly.

"I mean I've never done it before, but I'll try anything once," She said anxiously as she stood up, revealing her perfect body.

"Jesus Christ, Ray told me you were sexy but this is just insane," Phil said as he gawked at Erin's figure.

"Why don't you two doctors get over here and prescribe me some big, hard medicine?" She said as she spanked her own ass.

It didn't take much convincing for Ray and Phil to immediately begin pleasuring Erin. Phil sucked her supple breasts as Ray began eating her delicious pussy. Erin had never felt so dirty, but she loved it. Having two grown men at her disposal. These rich doctors were tied around her finger and they would do whatever she said. Erin pushed the men off of her, stood up and then bent over.

"I want one of you to lick my pussy while the other eats my ass," She demanded. Within no time at all, Phil was devouring her vagina and Ray was licking her asshole with a passion. She loved the control she had! Next, Erin ordered that both doctors get completely naked. She was surprised to see that Phil's penis was significantly smaller than Ray's, but she figured it would be a perfect fit for her ass. She pushed Ray into a chair and announced her next demand

"Doctor Stone, I want to ride your cock. Doctor Cantro I want you to fuck me in the ass," She said authoritatively. She mounted Ray who was still sitting in the chair and began to bounce up and down on his rock hard member. Phil went into a nearby drawer and grabbed some lubricant. He lubed his cock up and headed back over to the action.

"Hold still you two," He said as he guided his penis towards Erin's ass. He eased his way in and Erin let out a high-pitched scream. After it was in, Erin felt amazing. She felt so incredibly full, two doctor cocks in her at the same time.

"Now fuck me hard and fast boys," She yelled. Ray and Phil began relentlessly pounding her. Every time she would bounce to the top of Ray's rod she would feel Phil's dick penetrating her asshole. She was in a state of complete ecstasy, being completely manhandled and stretched. She felt like an animal, an animal that was about to be ripped in two. Her orgasm came quickly and with an unrivaled intensity. Eventually she made her way to the floor and got on her hands and knees. Phil continued punishing her from the rear. Ray stood up in front of her and she began deep-throating his cock. She sucked him hard as she continued to moan in pleasure, Phil's cock still pleasuring her asshole intensely.

"God you're such a dirty girl," Phil said as he pulled his dick in and out of her ass, watching it stretch each time he re-entered.

"Suck that cock, baby," Ray said as he rolled his head back in pleasure. "Oh yeah, that's it. You're going to make me cum," He continued.

"I want you both to cum for me," Erin said as moved forward, removing Phil's member from her bum. She hopped up on the table and began fingering herself.

"Doctor Stone, Doctor Cantro, I want my medicine now," She said as she opened her mouth and continued fingering her moist pussy. Ray and Phil knew exactly what she wanted so they began to stroke their cocks as they made their way over to the table. Erin waited in anticipation as the two doctors prepared to give her their loads.

"Come on doctors, give me what I want. Cover me in your steaming hot cum!" She yelled. Ray and Phil were on opposite sides of the table and they were both pointing their cocks directly at Erin as they continued to stroke themselves. They were grunting and groaning and Erin knew they were close. She closed her eyes and continued masturbating. Within no time she could feel herself cumming again. She was excited for what was to come.

"Open wide," Ray said before he started shooting his load. Phil was not far behind Erin opened her mouth and stuck out her tongue just as both men ejaculated. She could feel the warm cum squirting all over her, first on her breasts, then on her face and in her mouth. It was so warm and creamy and she embraced it fully. Before long her mouth was full of cum. All she could hear were the sounds of both men moaning in pleasure as they emptied their balls all over Erin's cute face.

"Swallow that down baby," Phil said. Erin drank it down and then started wiping off her face. As she opened her eyes she could see the big smiles on both of the doctors faces. She knew they loved what she had just done. Ray threw her a towel to clean up and she rinsed her face off in a nearby sink. She threw her clothes back on and grabbed her purse. She had never felt so fulfilled; she had just made two men have incredible orgasms and she herself had had the best one of her entire life.

"Same time next week boys?" She asked, trying not to seem too desperate.

"Yes!" They replied in unison.

She couldn't wait for her next appointment. She left the medical center and immediately called Cassandra; needless to say she was thoroughly impressed with Erin's conquest.

I hope this book provided you with some great XXX entertainment and some fantastic pleasure. If you enjoyed it, then I really think you will enjoy another one of my steamy hot titles. Check out the sample on the following pages and let your imagination run wild!

Sincerely,

Everlette Saunders

FORBIDDEN PLEASURES

Begging My Professor For The A

My Naughty Backdoor Fantasy

Everlette Saunders

Table Of Contents

Chapter 1: Leanna & Johnny

"That's exactly what I want Johnny, Oh yes... yes." Leanna quickly covered her hand with her mouth as she looked down to watch her boyfriend's head moving vigorously between her thighs.

Normally she wouldn't care, being loud was part of the fun, and she liked to express herself, but tonight they were at a frat party, and as much as she would love to make sure everyone knew what was happening in the laundry room, she needed to find release more. She was currently leaning back on the washing machine with one foot planted on the top and the other hanging down. She was resting on her elbows so that should watch his head moving. She loved to watch him in action. She felt his fingers probing her roughly. Gone was any idea of being soft or careful. She was wet, swollen and aching. Johnny was always such a giver and she loved getting him riled up. It all started when they first arrived at the party.

They always played this game where they would pick out the hottest woman in the room and talk about who would have her first, and how. Tonight had been a beautiful blonde. Petite in the waist with huge breasts, she had been the perfect one to point out to him. She knew he always liked a woman with a nice rack. He immediately chimed in as they played out the fantasy verbally. They had both been hot and ready when they found their way to this room. There were slits in the folds in the door so anyone could see if they happened to pass by, part of the thrill for her. Johnny had described how much he wanted to pump into both her and the little blonde over and over, back and forth between the two. Thinking of it again now pushed her over the edge and into the sweet oblivion that she needed.

"That's it don't you stop Johnny, side to side, yes yes." She moaned loudly, grinding into his face as the wave hit her.

He knew her body well enough to know she was sated and immediately pulled her, scooting her forward until she was slightly hanging off of the machine. He moved and pushed into her roughly, slamming and banging. She loved the roughness and always wanted more, but Johnny wasn't as into it as she was. She laid flat on her back to give him better access and she moaned as she felt him deeper than before. He was average in size, but he made up for it in his eagerness to please.

She felt him push into her longer and slower and she knew he was nearing release. This was the best time to ask for what she really wanted.

"Johnny baby, take me the other way, the way I really want." She begged him, knowing he loved when she begged. He looked up at her and swore as he found release. When it was over he smiled at her.

"You're so good baby, I love when you beg I can't help it... besides we've talked about that. You know how I feel about it, it's just not something I'm into." He helped her stand and gave her a kiss. She kissed him back.

Chapter 2: Wanting More, Needing More

She always wanted more, more especially than he was willing to give. They had been together for two years. Both eager to please one another and both enjoying a very active sex life. They were good for each other, both giving and sharing, until lately. She wanted him to explore her more and give her more. She wanted him to try anal just once, but he didn't want to. She knew that it would be a challenge. It would take time to ease into it, but it was something they could do together, an adventure of sorts. She was begging to give him every orifice on her body and he always said no. She had purchased several toys to use on that passage and no matter what she tried he would always rush into getting it done, leaving her even more curious. He was turned on by her using them on herself, working both areas at once, but he wanted no part in doing it himself. She straightened her clothes and followed him back out to the party.

She had to wonder if this relationship was really working for them both or simply him alone. She crossed her arms as he went to get them both a drink. Usually she orgasmed two if not three times and lately, she was lucky to get one. Everything with him was rushed and what she wanted was something long and drawn out. She knew that things would change the longer they were together, but she was completely unfulfilled, and it wasn't fair. The party went on for another hour or so and Johnny was engaged in a lengthy battle about some football team with his friends. She took a stroll outside to feel some fresh air and that's when she saw someone move towards the pool house.

Normally she wasn't that concerned about what people did, or who they did it with but she was almost positive it had been the blonde, the target of their focus previously that evening. She walked slowly towards the pool house and slid up to the window to peer inside. What she saw made her smile. Sure enough the hot blonde from earlier that evening was laid out on the couch inside and someone was between her thick thighs kissing her delicately. She was a hot one, they had been right about that. She was roughly massaging her own ample breast in her hands tweaking the nipples as she whimpered at the job the unseen man was doing to her. She took a step closer to see more of the room. She was in the doorway before she knew it and the blonde saw her standing there. There was something about the blonde lying there staring back at Leanna that made her feel the slow heat building back up again. She probably should have left the scene, but it was too hot watching them.

Made in the USA
Coppell, TX
27 May 2021

56429018R00026